Too Hot to S...

Written and illustrated by Steve Webb

Collins

In the desert in the East where the sand is so hot, Hoppitt the Gazelle likes to hop, hop, hop!

Come and meet his friends in the desert sun.
Hop along with Hoppitt, the day has just begun!

The sand cat sat by the cactus tree.

"Come on, sand cat, come with me!"

The camel is a mammal with a hump upon his back.

"Follow us!" said the sand cat. "Follow our track."

"What's the hurry, Hoppitt?" asked the lizard in the shade.

"Won't you stop it, Hoppitt?" said the fox on the rocks.

10

"Too hot to stop!" said the camel and the cat.
"Too hot to stop!" said the lizard at the back.

"Sss-stop it, Hoppitt, sss-stop it," hissed the snake on a dune.
"If you're hopping up there, you'd better stop soon."

"Stop it, Hoppitt, stop it," warned the falcon, flying by.
"I can see where you're heading, from high up in the sky."

Hoppitt hopped up the sand dune, so tall and so wide.

When he got to the top, he hopped off the other side …

SPLASH!

A lake full of water, so deep and so cool,
Hoppitt splashed down into the desert pool.

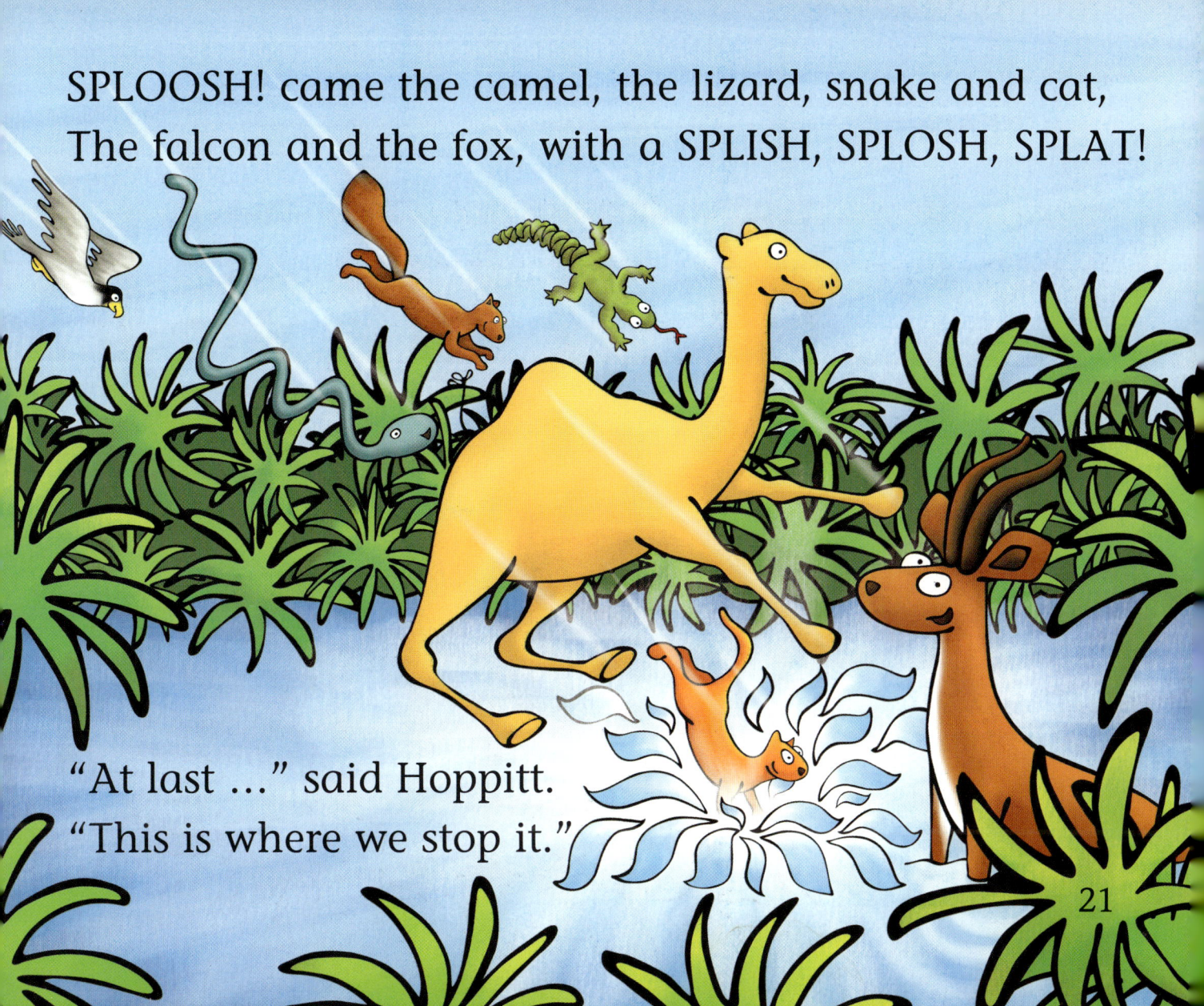

Ideas for reading

Written by Clare Dowdall, PhD
Lecturer and Primary Literacy Consultant

Reading objectives:
- discuss the significance of the title and events
- learn to appreciate rhymes and poems, and to recite some by heart
- predict what might happen on the basis of what has been read so far
- apply phonic knowledge and skills as the route to decode words
- explain clearly their understanding of what is read to them

Spoken language objectives:
- use spoken language to develop understanding through speculating, hypothesising, imagining and exploring ideas
- participate in discussions and performances
- speak audibly and fluently with an increasing command of Standard English
- listen and respond appropriately to adults and their peers

Curriculum links: Science; Geography

High frequency words: too, to, where, so, his, just, with, our, what, little, when

Interest words: desert, east, gazelle, cactus, camel, mammal, track, lizard, parade, dune, falcon, splosh

Word count: 243

Resources: magnetic letters and board, ICT

Build a context for reading

- Look at the front cover together. Read the words and discuss what type of animal is shown, and where he is. Children may not know *gazelle*, so list their suggestions.

- Look at the title *Too Hot to Stop!* Notice the high frequency word *too* and its spelling and meaning. Ask children to think of other words with an *oo* digraph and the same phoneme, e.g. room, zoo, hoop.

- Read the blurb on the back cover together, and ask children to choose words that rhyme, e.g. hop and stop. Check they do not think that hot and stop rhyme. Use magnetic letters to make other words that rhyme with hop and stop.

Understand and apply reading strategies

- Introduce the interest words that appear in the book, e.g. dune. Help children to read them aloud and become familiar with them.

- Read the poem together to p5. Ask them to predict what is going to happen to Hoppitt and the sand cat next. Ask who they might meet and what they might do.